Bracknell Forest Council

Goo oose

Ad ox

To avoid overdue charges this book should be returned on
or before the last date stamped above. If not required by
another reader it may be renewed in person, by telephone,
post or on-line at www.bracknell-forest.gov.uk/libraries

Library & Information Service

5430000522027 1

D1380291

Designed by Helen Cooke
Edited by Jenny Tyler and Lesley Sims
Reading consultants: Alison Kelly and Anne Washtell

There is a little yellow duck to find on every page.

"Woo-hoo!" shouts Goose.
She's on the loose.

Her horn honks loudly...

TOOT!

TOOT!

TOOT!

"Slow down!" says Hen.
"Don't go so fast."

Goose sounds her horn
as she zooms past.

Ted's out planting,
by his shed...

...then Goose heads through his flowerbed!

Toad's moving bricks
along the road.

Goose makes Toad brake.

There goes my load!

Scared pigeons "Coo!"
and cows go "Moo!"

"Slow down," scowls Owl,
with a "twit-twoo!"

Goose rides her scooter
to the zoo...

...through kangaroos...

...and cockatoos.

"That foolish Goose has got to stop."

They hear a screech,
a shriek and...

Now look at Goose in Penguin's pool!

That's ended all her fun.

"I feel so foolish," splutters Goose.
"My racing days are done."

Puzzles

Puzzle 1

Can you find the
words that rhyme?

Goose	load
fast	fool
road	shed
pool	loose
Ted	past

Puzzle 2

One word is wrong in this speech bubble.
What should it say?

I feed so
foolish!

Puzzle 3
Can you find these things in the picture?

Goose   pigeons

Owl   scooter

cows   branch

Puzzle 4
Choose the right speech bubble for the picture.

Slow down!

Go down!

Answers to puzzles

Puzzle 1

Goose ⟶ loose

fast ⟶ past

road ⟶ load

pool ⟶ fool

Ted ⟶ shed

Puzzle 2

I <u>feel</u> so foolish!

Puzzle 3

cows

Owl

branch

Goose

scooter

pigeons

Puzzle 4

Slow down!

About phonics

Phonics is a method of teaching reading used extensively in today's schools. At its heart is an emphasis on identifying the *sounds* of letters, or combinations of letters, that are then put together to make words. These sounds are known as phonemes.

Starting to read

Learning to read is an important milestone for any child. The process can begin well before children start to learn letters and put them together to read words. The sooner children can discover books and enjoy stories and language, the better they will be prepared for reading themselves, first with the help of an adult and then independently.

You can find out more about phonics on the Usborne Very First Reading website, **usborne.com/veryfirstreading** (US readers go to **veryfirstreading.com**). Click on the **Parents** tab at the top of the page, then scroll down and click on **About synthetic phonics**.

Phonemic awareness

An important early stage in pre-reading and early reading is developing phonemic awareness: that is, listening out for the sounds within words. Rhymes, rhyming stories and alliteration are excellent ways of encouraging phonemic awareness.

In this story, your child will soon identify the *oo* sound, as in **goose** and **loose**. Look out, too, for rhymes such as **fast** – **past** and **road** – **load**.

Hearing your child read

If your child is reading a story to you, don't rush to correct mistakes, but be ready to prompt or guide if he or she is struggling. Above all, give plenty of praise and encouragement.

TOOT!
TOOT!